eBook ISBN: 978-1-7391461-3-9
Paper back: ISBN-13: 978-1-7391461-2-2

Cover design by Frank Prendergast
https://www.frankandmarci.com

Important note

This story depicts sleep disorders and medical conditions. If you have concerns about your sleep or health, consult a qualified medical practitioner – ideally a sleep-trained healthcare professional. Do not change your medication without discussing it with your physician first, as this could worsen your condition.

When to seek medical advice

Consult a sleep-trained healthcare professional if you can't sleep, keep falling asleep, or something happens that you don't like when you go to sleep. They can assess your symptoms and recommend appropriate treatment options.

Prioritise your well-being

Poor sleep can significantly impact your health and quality of life. If sleep disturbances interfere with your daily functioning, seek guidance from a healthcare provider specialising in sleep medicine to identify the cause and develop a personalized treatment plan.

Donations

A contribution from the proceeds of the sale of this book will be donated to the British Society of Pharmacy Sleep Services and the Sleep Charity.

PROLOGUE

The US President kicks off their second term with a trade war against China, setting off a cascade of unforeseen events around the world.

With the loss of a key trade partner and a significant revenue stream, China turns to its clamouring "friend," Russia. Russia steps in to buy what the US will not, with Chinese annexation of Mongolia the price of the bride.

Feeling slighted on the world stage, China redoubles its internal and regional ambitions. Its grip on Hong Kong tightens, hostility towards Taiwan escalates, and tensions in the South China Sea transform the region into a seething flashpoint. A coordinated US led naval and airborne response only increases the pressure and risk of direct confrontation.

Sensing global distraction, Houthi rebels seize the moment to expand their maritime piracy. More international shipping is hijacked, as maritime defences amount to zero, sending Lloyd's of London insurance rates soaring and crippling global logistics.

Meanwhile, EU sanctions on Russian oil unintentionally intensify the Russo-China alliance. Resupplied with Chinese electronics and emboldened by its new superpower partner, Russia ramps up its campaign in Ukraine, forcing the EU to hike taxes to secure oil on the increasingly expensive global market. OPEC seizes the moment, raising barrel prices to record highs as Arab nations coalesce and escalate hostilities towards Israel.

An increasingly isolated NATO, weakened without robust US support, looks on impotently as Russian rhetoric gets louder. North Korean troops mass along the Russo-Finnish border while Iranian drone technology continues to evolve, becoming cheaper, deadlier, and more prolific.

Russo-China cyber warfare intensifies. Exploiting dark web data breaches and hiding behind encrypted communications, social media platforms and AI companies, they destabilise trust in online commerce. Amazon falters under the pressure, and the stock market suffers a catastrophic crash - twice. Amid the chaos, Warren Buffett and Berkshire Hathaway grow ever richer.

In the shadows, Chinese pharmaceutical labs use AI to engineer increasingly potent nitazene derivatives. Many hundreds of times more powerful than fentanyl. State backed Triad/Bratva begin distribution of counterfeit medicines. The result is an unprecedented wave of crime that sweeps across continents.

Desiring ever great wealth, criminal gangs recognise the enormous potential of the insomnia market. Now estimated at 1 in 3 adults. They contaminate 'sleep aids' with the newly developed nitazene derivatives to reach a new and previously untapped market. Penetrating grey markets for legitimate medicines they distribute counterfeit, nitazene contaminated 'sleep aids'.

What began as a tidal wave of insomniac addiction and associated crime to support it, mutates into a full-blown tsunami of crime.

The Russian leader was so impassioned, his spittle hit the microphone, *"Destroy the West while they try to sleep. Turn them upon themselves. Eliminate police IT systems and stretch their meagre military by enforcing curfews. Break their spirit. They will be unable to respond as the US is looking inward. NATOs power wiped away. We will rise and crush them"*.

In China, the party secretary was equally emotional, though culturally more restrained, in his statement that echoed the Russian speech. *"We will help them sleep"*.

In Europe, the newly imposed and crippling taxes are widely ignored. In a surprising move the EU announces a retirement age reduction.

Disillusioned citizens seize the updated retirement age of 45 and emigration on a vast scale begins. An entire generation head south to retire in Greece, Italy,

Portugal or Spain, where they're met with resentment from locals struggling with colossal debts, no sleep, and no future.

CHAPTER ONE

"Dodging bloody turds". That's how I'd describe it. Gotta open up drains again.

I don't mind the work. Arrr, I know it's not everyone's cup of tea, but I don't mind it. Everyone goes after all.

"Oooh. Here it comes."

The cop standing beside him watches as he bends down, then scoops out assorted, unidentifiable 'stuff'. Plop, splatter, plop, as it drops into a previously immaculate white plastic bucket, held by a lab tech.

About a minute earlier, the police surrounded the house, in a coordinated swoop. Rammed the door and shouted as they went from room to room.

Outside, the drains guy was 'Dodging turds' for drugs the occupants flushed down the toilet.

Electric cars help with this. Pete had turned off the 'spaceship' sound effects and arrived silently. Another drug bust. Stealthy until it's not.

The place was a neglected house, in a neglected street, in a neglected part of town. Rubbish lay strewn in the street; over what had been the front garden; and everywhere inside the house. Pete stepped carefully around things as much as possible. Rounding up the druggies. It was all planned and well-practiced.

Pete was 6 foot 10 inches tall. And unlike most tall people Pete wasn't thin or stooped. His admirers would describe him as 'well-muscled'. And at 40 he worked hard to stay in shape.

"In position. Go!" Came over his earpiece. Pete nodded at the guy holding the door ram and crash the door swung free – in they went. No need to run. All the exits were covered.

The smell hit him first.

Dead body.

Unmistakable.

As Pete stepped over and around comatose bodies, lying like blown leaves, he tread carefully. A needle stick injury was the last thing he needed.

And Bill 'the drains guy', in position, waited for his delivery.

"What's your name?"

"Shaun" he mumbled like his mouth didn't work.

"What's your last name?"

"Hayes".

"Shaun, I'm Detective Pete Schmitt do you understand your rights as I've explained them to you?"

"Errr yeah…" he slurs.

"Do you know who the dead woman is?"

"Helen", Shaun blurts and dissolves into tears.

What a mess. This guy looks like he hasn't eaten in a month. Smells like he hasn't washed in a month too.

"Shaun, do you know how she died?"

Detective Peter Schmitt. Blonde, blue eyes, 40 years old and tall. Really tall. No kids, a mortgage and an ex-wife. Pete was both unusual and usual. Unusual in size; his physical presence got some cops backs up, usual in that he was divorced, because he was married to the job.

Thinking back, now sat at his desk, chair creaking, Pete had known this drugs raid was coming for a while. It was routine. Even finding one dead was normal. He wondered if they'd be able to identify the deceased. That was sometimes a problem. The only guy vaguely conscious at the scene was a blubbering wreck. Across town the coroner had been notified, and the path lab was ready.

Ready to receive.

A one-way journey.

'I really miss him'. Sameera was thinking about her son. It seemed such a long time since she'd seen him. She hoped he was ok.

What seemed a lifetime ago she'd been a pharmacist. Now she was a coroner, proud to say how her pharmacy background opened up so many opportunities. And there was no fooling her on the toxicology reports.

She'd been notified about the deceased and didn't need to attend the drugs bust scene. The forensic pathologist had it under control.

Another overdose.

Nothing to see here.

Move along.

"It was just a few 'sleep aids'. Nothing... We'd taken them loads of times before. Just a 'sleep aid'. Everyone took 'em. How can she be dead?"

Arrested.

For possession and I'm facing time inside. I should feel something. But I'm numb. Crashing. I'd reach for the 'sleep aids' but then the memories came crashing back *"Oh shit, Helen's dead"*. I gave her some of the 'sleep aids' I bought online. But I told her they knocked me out. Were way stronger than stuff I bought pharming the town chemists. I guess she didn't believe me.

Thought I was a lightweight.

Now she's dead.

I'm so tired. So low. Can't think. Drained of emotion.

"Shaun, I am arresting you on suspicion of possession of a controlled substance with intent to supply. You do not have to....."

I zoned out then.

The big, blonde, hairy ape scared me.

Not his words.

The unreal size of the guy.

CHAPTER TWO

Life was about to get complicated for Sameera. But she didn't know it yet. She'd not seen or heard from Shaun, for some time.

Shaun was at university studying Modern History and she was having to let him find his feet. Her only child. Not easy.

The sudden rumble of her muted phone, vibrating on her desk, dragged her mind back to the job.

"Coroner's office. Sameera speaking".

Pete identified himself and continued to explain that he was calling 'off the record' as a professional courtesy.

He'd just arrested her son.

"What's the extra pill?", a new one had appeared in her evening pill pot that she didn't recognise. They told her it was for her pain and inflammation. Doris wasn't convinced. The first week passed and she complied and took the pills.

Her arm hurt. Not so badly now it was in a sling, and it was fine if she didn't move it. Doris had tripped in her home and because she was in her 90s and lived alone, they'd arranged to get her temporarily (she hoped), into a care home.

Doris was all there. 100%. In her weekly mahjong and scrabble clubs, she was known as a fierce competitor. Frail for sure but her mind was sharp. She knew what was going on in the world too. Her Sunday broadsheet kept her well informed.

In the care home, she ate better than she did alone, and as the first week ended and the second began it was odd that she felt increasingly woolly in the morning. She found herself more wobbly on her feet too. They tried to keep her from moving around expressing their fear of her falling again. But by afternoon her head would clear and up she'd get going walking up and down the corridor with her stick.

Fate took a turn, when she fumbled the white paper pill pot one evening, and the contents scattered across her side table. She rounded them up and swallowed them with a sip of tea. No drama.

Except she'd missed one.

The extra one that had rolled under her folded newspaper. In the morning, she woke feeling much clearer than she had of late. So, when she tidied the table ready for breakfast and found the extra pill, she immediately glanced at her arm.

No swelling.

Flickering, almost painfully bright, UV light, reflecting from multiple, clear glass containers of various sizes. A lot of glass. Glass doors on cupboards, but no windows. An electric hum from something. Maybe the lights. Maybe the refrigeration.

The path lab was deep inside the building. Only the 'paper pushers', had windows. The chance someone might see what went on inside the path lab, and the need to control the environment, dictated no windows.

They'd identified the drugs, Bill recovered, that had been flushed down the loo. Heroin and two of the commonly abused 'sleep aids', Diphenhydramine Hydrochloride and Promethazine.

And something else. An insanely powerful drug.

It all went down on the report in cold, dispassionate, black and white terms.

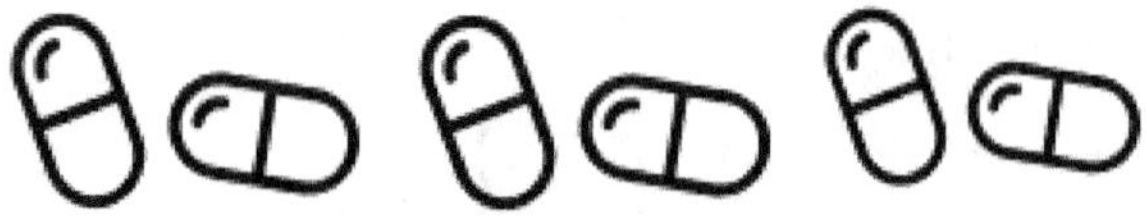

"Ain't no cup holders in my car. 1996. They made cars properly then. It weren't all plastic like now".

Bill 'the drains guy' loved his old Volvo. He'd bought it after it had sat unused for several years in a care home car park. No one thought he'd get it going again- let alone turn it into the family everyday car.

"Ahh. Brought my newborn daughter home from hospital in that car. Hah! Could have done with a bloody coffee then!"

Reflecting on how everyone these days went about propped up with giant cups of coffee or cans of 'energy' drink, made Bill wonder: are we more tired these days or did we get better and more sleep in the late 1990s, and not need cup holders in our cars?

"Shoot him! Oh you missed. Get 'im!"

"Which one? There's so many..."

"The Zombie! Theo. Look! He's coming right at yah".

I blew the Zombie away. And countless others. I was a strange sight, prancing around my front room in just my pants, VR goggles strapped to my head. The other child player, shouting as he and I battled the undead horde.

Then it struck me.

'When I was sleepwalking, did I look like a Zombie?' They said I'd grow out of it; it was just a phase.

I wasn't so sure.

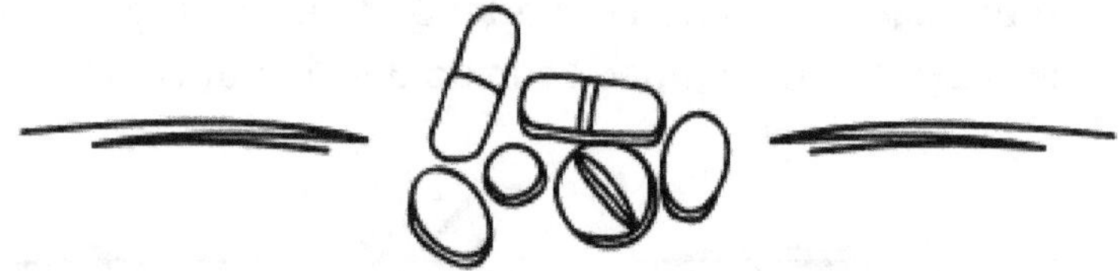

'What to do about them? Sleep aids. They seem to fly below the radar somehow. An open secret. It's like they're too big a problem to tackle'.

Pete's subconscious worked the problem. When he ran, he found that sometimes the pieces dropped into place. It was as if he needed the time away to process things.

This morning, as he ran in the dark, beyond the 'toxic 10', and his breathing settled into a steady rhythm, he wondered what it would take for 'sleep aids' to be more difficult to obtain?

Then it occurred to him. Sameera would know. Not just because he'd just arrested her son, but because she'd been a pharmacist.

'I wonder if she'd be open to a little chat about it?'

Shaun was not a happy young man. And neither was his Mum.

Sameera Hayes the coroner, was quite well-known in the police station. Her job necessarily involved her in close liaison with the police. Certain officers nodded when they saw her in passing through the corridors. It was that sort of relationship.

But now her son had put her in an awkward situation. Both mother, son and the police knew it.

When Pete entered the interview room with his colleague, he caught her eye, but didn't smile.

It was like that.

"Hello Shaun. I'm Detective Pete Schmitt and this is my colleague sergeant Emily Watts. We've met before. Do you recall?"

"Not really" replied Shaun. He'd sobered up some with the shock of it all and the mixture of contempt and pity shown by his mother.

"Hi Sameera, this interview is being recorded and I must remind you both that Shaun you're under caution. Do you understand?"

"Ok". Replied Shaun.

"Shaun, I arrested you this morning for drugs offences. We'll come to those later, but I wanted to ask you about Helen. The dead woman you identified in the house. Do you recall?"

"Yeah", Shaun nodded.

"Shaun, do you know how she died?"

The interview progressed and Shaun cooperated. He explained as much as he could remember, until Pete felt he had to call the doctor because Shaun's lack of sleep, near starvation, shock and dehydration threatened to overwhelm him.

"Interview suspended…" Sameera went to leave with her son and the paramedics. But Pete asked her to wait and said turning to Emily, *"Could you get us some coffee?"* Which meant 'take a while'.

Pete stopping the recording, looked up and faced Sameera.

"Sameera, we have a problem. In fact, you have a problem". He emphasised the 'you' by pointing his finger at her.

"I have to charge Shaun for possession", he said looking up at the ceiling. *"The issue is complicated*

because we have a death and Shaun admitted he supplied Helen with 'sleep aids'".

"Sleep aids aren't prescription meds..." replied Sameera her voice trailing off. Realising how lame it sounded, and regretting having spoken. Followed by,

"Let's see what the tox screen says".

"Yeah, OK. How long?"

"I will expedite it."

Pete thought, 'Yeah, I bet you will'.

CHAPTER THREE

Doris felt a bit naughty. And that was fun at first. She deliberately avoided taking THAT pill and she found herself less foggy in the morning and a lot less likely to fall. Which became a virtuous circle, in that her confidence moving about returned.

Over the course of the next month, she flushed THAT pill down the toilet every evening. Her arm was almost fully recovered.

During that month, she kept her peace. But she watched and she made covert notes in a meticulous fashion in a notebook hidden in her broadsheet newspaper. As much as anything, to keep herself amused. Maybe she was just imagining it. Could it really be true?

Doris recorded resident's names, times and changes in their behaviour, after they had their medication. What she witnessed concerned her greatly. It appeared a systematic process of sedating the care home residents. Seemingly to keep them subdued and easier to 'care' for.

One afternoon, she struck upon an ironic title for her notebook:

'The Don't Care Home'. I should be a novelist she smiled to herself.

"Sameera, I'm wondering if we can help each other?"

Pete pretended to be deep in thought, as he stroked his chin.

Sameera looked him straight in the eye but said nothing.

"Abuse of 'sleep aids' is a big and growing problem. I want to know if you'll help me".

Pete stopped. Nothing more to be said.

Sameera merely nodded once.

The coffee arrived.

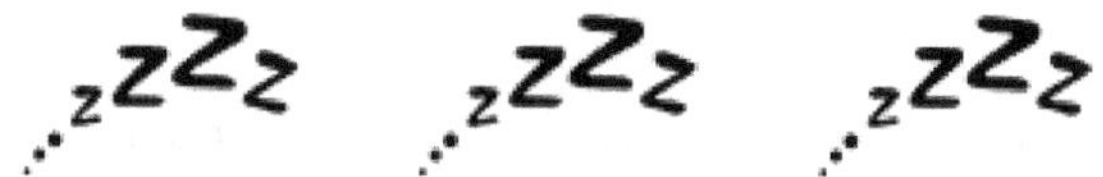

"You look silly".

"Go away Katie", I growled.

"Theo is silly!" She threw back at me. My little sister is winding me up.

"What do you want Katie?"

"Play with me", she replied.

"Zombie's – arghhh – get them", came over the speaker of my VR headset. And with that Katie walked away, to play Teddy School, on her own.

My parents limit my screen time. Well attempt to. But it seems to them it's all I ever want to do. They don't get it. I meet my friends there and we play together.

They only ever seem to limit me. It's not fair...

'I've got to be quiet as Mummy is on a call'. Katie whined to herself.

Katie wished Theo would come and play. So she stomped her little legs up the stairs to the landing. Then a thought occurred to her.

So, she went into 'stealth mode' as only little kids can and pushed open Mummy and Daddy's bedroom door. Silently, she started exploring all the forbidden areas of her parents' bedroom.

Downstairs, she could hear her brother and his friend, continuing to shout at each other. On the other side of their house, she knew Mummy had the doors shut, so her customers didn't have to endure 'Zombie Apocalypse 33'. Which meant she had time and was unlikely to be overheard.

She pulled Mummy's top draw open and looked inside. 'Sweeties!' Thought Katie. In little pots and in strips with shiny, silvery foil. Ignoring the other items that would make her Mummy curl up with embarrassment, Katie took the 'sweeties' and sat on her parents' bed. She'd tried to open these sweetie pots before. They were tricky.

But this time Mummy hadn't quite put the lid on properly. And 'ohh no! I've spilt them all over the bed'.

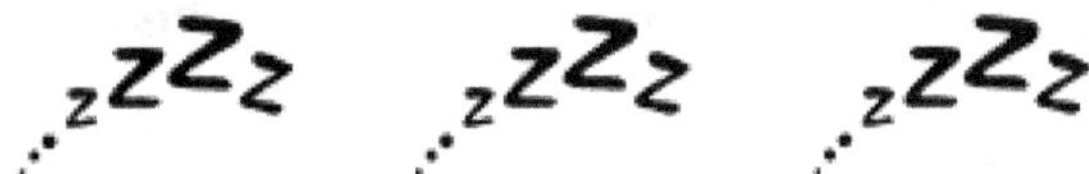

"Theo. Where's your sister?.... Theo, I'm talking to you". His Mum said.

The Zombie horde surged forward. He needed to reload.

"Dunno". Was the ever-helpful reply. Theo was in another world.

Turning away, *"Katie!"* Shouted Emma. Again, and again. Increasing in volume and then anxiety when there was still no reply.

"KATIE!" And Emma started running. Desperately searching and shouting. Living every parent's nightmare. A lost child. Yet, in the back of her mind she half expected Katie to come out of a room in some costume or other, and she'd have to swallow the fear and play along as if nothing had happened.

But Katie didn't appear.

Searching from room to room, Emma finally burst into her own bedroom, and on seeing Katie went cold with dread. Her little angel girl was unconscious, and limp lying on the bed with vomit in her hair, surrounded by pills. A scene that would forever be etched in her mind.

She had a pulse.

She was still alive.

Snatching her up, Emma somehow appeared downstairs in the kitchen a moment later, calling emergency services.

The Zombies kept coming.

CHAPTER FOUR

It was always a sombre time when a resident died.
There was a peculiar silence. Oppressive, all pervading,
like a liquid spreading through the building.

Depending on your viewpoint, it was either good or
bad that the silence didn't last long. Silence
punctuated by the groaning of those in the final stages
of dementia.

A chill went through Doris.

Was it better to lose your physical health and be aware
of it? She shivered and straightened the blanket over
her knees.
'I want to go home now' she thought.

Her 'Don't Care Home' notebook, now in its second
month of annotations, was quite comprehensive. The
recently deceased appeared within.

But what to do?

"Emergency Services. Which service do you require?"

"Ambulance," Emma replied. Clinging to Katie. Wishing her husband would come home...

"Ambulance service".

And before Emma could speak the operator cut in with her phone number for the handover to the ambulance service and the recording. When Emma finally got to speak, her words came out in sobs.

Katie was a rag doll in her arms.

Scoop and dash on Blues and Twos. In the ambulance the paramedics fought for Katie's life. While Emma wanted to die with every type of recrimination raging through her mind.

"Pick up the phone!" Her husband wasn't answering. While Theo continued battling Zombies, the life in his headset slowly draining away, the battery indicator began flashing red.

Almost dead.

Doris's house was immaculately clean. As her son stood in the kitchen clutching the bin bag, looking about him, he was impressed.

He'd done a small grocery shop and replaced the mouldy contents of her fridge. Folded up the multiple, large newspapers and put them, together with presumably a few utility bills, on the kitchen table. Now fumbling, one-handed with the door handle, the son let himself out and drove to the "Don't Care Home".

Doris was coming home.

"Oh hell. Why did you call the police?" She said.

The police would have lots of questions. Emma was having a really bad day.

"The details surrounding Katie's consumption of pills raise concerns about her safety". The nurse replied.

There wasn't a lot of arguing with that.

While the early signs for Katie looked good because she'd vomited, she was unconscious, on a drip and intubated. Not out of the woods yet.

Katie had eaten mummy's anti-depressants, oral contraceptive and insomnia pills. 'Sleep aids' as they were commonly known.

Social services were inbound. Time and the police would determine the family's future.

You couldn't make it up.

Sameera's conflict of interest about her son and the death of Helen, gave her sleepless nights. Yet, as a coroner she was not to withdraw herself from a situation lightly.

She resolved to escalate this and seek advice. If she played it right, it could get Detective Schmitt's "claws" out of her. Though she recognised a fine line was to be walked, as at least appearing to help Schmitt might help her son.

Family, integrity, professionalism, and her reputation.
All competing.

*"What's remotely suspicious about a care home
resident dying?"* Mused Pete as he drove across town
to the coroner's office. 'Why am I getting involved?

Wasn't it expected – we get old and die?'

But Sameera had called Pete with a bizarre story,
about seemingly contaminated 'sleep aids'. So, despite
himself he was intrigued.

Sameera had ordered a toxicology test to be carried
out upon the deceased, as a care home resident had
called her office, and now she wanted to share the test
results.

Doris clearly wasn't stupid.

The husband returns home; still in a conference call in his car, he sits outside for half an hour. Eventually he enters the house where he finds his son Theo, alone and hungry.

"Where's your Mum?"

"Dunno", he helpfully replies.

"And your sister? No..." holding up his hand, *"don't answer that. You don't know".*

Theo storm's upstairs and slams his bedroom door. Dad looks again at his phone and sees he has multiple new messages. It's late and he's trying to switch off from a tough day, so he presumes they're all work messages and decides they can wait until tomorrow. Emma has probably taken Katie to the local shops. A bit naughty to leave Theo on his own though. He's not yet 13. But she'll be back shortly no doubt.

Pouring a whisky, he thinks about dinner preparations and how long it will take for his son to return to earth. A knock at the door and glass in hand he opens the door to a police officer and a plainly dressed, middle-aged woman.

"Good evening, I'm PC Child and this is Mrs Blake from Social Services. Are you Mr Taylor?"

"Err. Yeah. Wha... what's this all about". Dad stutters in surprise.

"Can we come in?"

"Yeah... Yeah, please do. Come through". Dad beckons them through to the family's kitchen diner.

"What's this all about?" Mr Taylor repeats, slinging back his whisky.
"Have you spoken recently with your wife Sir?" The police officer queries in a slight condescending tone.

As if he should know at all times where his wife is.

"No. Not since this morning".

"Would you like to sit down Sir?

"You're worrying me know. Why don't you tell me why you're both here" Mr Taylor says, becoming anxious and a little irritated.

The police officer explains as objectively as possible. Trying hard not to convey an opinion one way or the other in his tone. Mrs Blake's face looks made of marble. Not a flicker of emotion.

Just then, Theo enters the kitchen and stops in surprise at the room's occupants. The mood of the room not entirely lost on him. He forgets his 'teenage' tantrum and goes to his dad for a hug.

The marble mask of Mrs Blake, for a fraction of a second cracks. A slight softening around her eyes, as she gently explains about Katie's overdose. This time, the explanation hits Mr Taylor hard. He's full of questions and wants to rush to Katie.

But why are Social Services here?

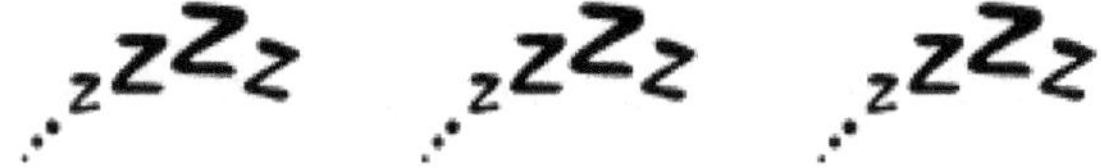

CHAPTER FIVE

"These are the facts," began Sameera, *"Helen's toxicology report reveals the presence of sedating antihistamines as expected..."*

Pete sighed and began to roll his eyes, *"and Nitazenes. Nothing else."*

"Nothing else?" He repeated incredulous.

"What's got me thinking though is the call the office took this morning. The local care home. A resident died. The caller alleges all sorts of nonsense, but a toxicology report shows the same sedating antihistamine and nitazene". Sameera went quiet.

Pete took a moment to process what she'd said. He picked up first Helen's report, and then beckoned Sameera to pass the other report, he compared it with the underlined section of the unnamed care home resident's report.

"I don't believe in coincidence", he said in a low voice.

"Let's talk to the caller about this. Something looks off".

Shaun continued staring at the wall in his police custody cell. While a flicker of perhaps hope, went through Sameera.

Doris was ready. Three cups and saucers all laid out. On hearing the doorbell, she flicked on the kettle and began shuffling her trolley to the front door. It took a few minutes for her to get there.

"Come in", she said. Not listening to them identify themselves. It didn't matter.

Over tea and biscuits, in high back chairs, Doris told her story. Detective Schmitt and Coroner Sameera Hayes went through emotions ranging from mildly curious to intrigued. Then Doris introduced her notebook, and a small, clear, plastic bag with a pill inside.

Pete leafed through the pages of her details. It was comprehensive. But what did it prove?

"I think we'd better pay the "Don't Care Home" a call".

"Is she going to be alright?" Dad asks the ICU nurse, who merely smiles world-weary eyes, and busies herself.

Emma reaches for his hand and the two of them are led away to a side room by the police officer and unsmiling woman from social services.

The conversation goes about as well as can be imagined. What was there to say? Yet the questions came and were answered. Again.

Yes, they loved their kids.

No, they weren't perfect.

Yes, they shouted at them on occasion and yes Theo had been in trouble at school. Yes, Dad worked late.

Yes, Mum screwed up not putting the lid on the bottle properly.

Guilt, remorse, tears, frustration. Resentment at being judged.

"Can you move 'em?"

"No problem boss," said the region level dealer. He wasn't about to disagree for fear of losing face. But he also knew it was a rhetorical question.

His job was to keep the money moving in the right direction. He was good at it, which was why he'd been given this extra job. More 'sleep aids.'

He'd found a new route to move them. A new customer group. He'd found a way into the insomnia market. It cost money but they made much more. And the volume he was able to move made him look good with his boss.

And the money flowed consistently in the right direction. Everyone was getting paid. Nobody was about to kill the golden goose.

Katie started fighting. She was waking up. Carefully, while monitoring her vital signs, they withdrew her ventilation. She breathed now with the aid of a non-invasive ventilator, purely as a backup measure. They were concerned she might relapse.

The hope was that no permanent liver damage had occurred.

Emma and her husband took alternating shifts. Being with Katie, being with Theo. Their respective employers were being understanding. One less thing to worry about. Grandparents were called, but they lived too far away to help and had their own health issues.

They were on their own.

For now, Social Services seem satisfied. They said they'd follow up and that hung over the pair, like a dark, forbidding cloud.

CHAPTER SIX

The tests on the 'sleep aid' Doris had given them came back. Nitazenes were present. Just like the tox report for Helen and the deceased from the care home.

Sameera was conflicted because her son was reportedly going 'cold turkey' in his police cell, they'd called an ambulance, and he'd been admitted.
Now she had two dead with nitazene on the tox reports. And Detective Schmitt sniffing around the care home.

While it appeared, Shaun hadn't knowingly killed Helen, he had admitted to giving her 'sleep aids'. 'Sleep aids' we now know that had been contaminated with nitazenes.

These 'sleep aids' where had Shaun got them? Did they get into the pharmacy supply chain? She needed to speak with Shaun.

Alone.

"....shot dead today..." Sameera turned up the car radio and listened to the details. It sounded like another drug related crime. Enforcers enforcing and the police clearing up.

The newsreader moved to the traffic report and Sameera switched it off.

She'd met again with Detective Schmitt, and they'd agreed to collaborate and pursue the source of the contaminated 'sleep aids'. He'd come across another case where nitazenes were involved, a young girl with an accidental overdose.

Still alive.

Schmitt said he'd bring her in on the blood test data, but it would be advisable to seek data sharing consent before she spoke with the parents. It was easier that way.

Were these 3 cases linked? Could this help Shaun, or would it implicate him further?

Sameera wasn't sleeping well.

Katie woke, sat up and pulled the ventilator mask off her head. She was thirsty, hungry, and wanted her teddy bear.

'Where's Mummy?'

'Where am I?'

They were treating Shaun for his dependency. He was one of the lucky ones, though he didn't feel like it. His Mum asked him question after question and when he was able, he answered as best he could. He wasn't much help as he'd been pharming the town's pharmacies, buying from dealers and online. It could have been anywhere.

When Sameera visited in her official coroner's capacity, with Detective Schmitt and Sergeant Watts, he saw his mum in a very different light.

Dealer's street names, where they could be found, and typically when, together with the website addresses and pharmacies, were all pieces of the picture Schmitt and his sidekick Emily recorded.

Shaun 'spilled his guts' to cooperate.

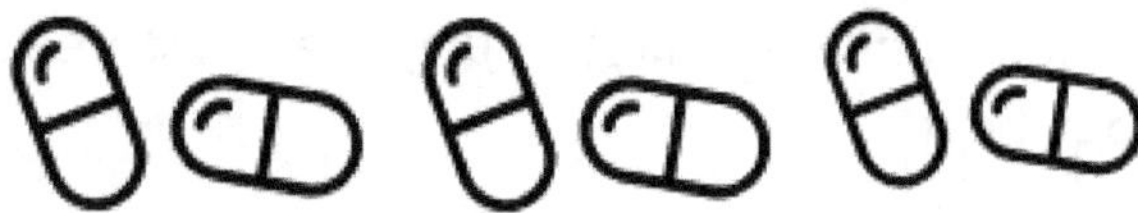

"Where's my money?"

"They did us over Boss. Triggers dead Boss", whined the dealer, in vain hope of mercy. He knew he was a dead man walking. Nobody loses that amount of cash and sees the sun come up the next morning.

But the boss wanted details of who'd robbed him. Who they worked for. Who was the enemy. It wasn't clear. He was guessing.

For now, the boss needed this man alive, as he was the route into the insomnia market regionally and perhaps nationally if he wasn't all talk.

So, he settled on just kneecapping him.

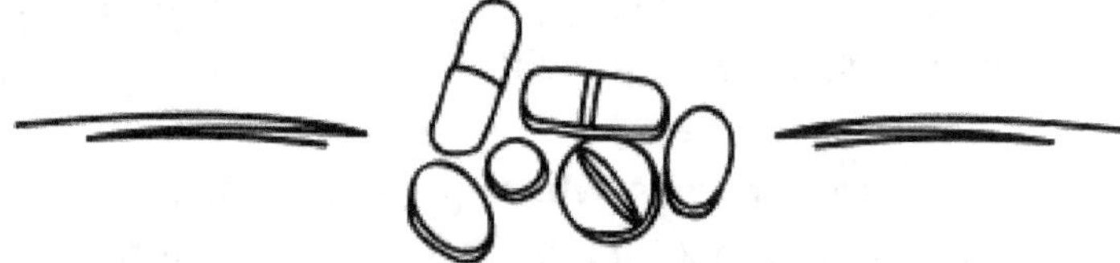

The care home was all a twitter. Doris was their hero! She'd uncovered an 'evil plot' to drug and kill them all.

Or so the buzz went.

Doris of course didn't play it down. It was the most fun she'd had in years.

The care home staff being somewhat less enthusiastic, had to arrange for the pharmacist to replace everyone's medication. Nobody trusted them. Everyone needed a medication review, and every pill had to be replaced.

Oddly enough, the residents were more chirpy the next morning.

THAT pill was not seen again.

Detective Pete Schmitt, had pieced the basics of the situation together, while out on his morning run. As he ran, he gnawed at the problem of who was behind this. And most importantly how were they getting this filth onto pharmacy shelves? That seem far-fetched. More plausible was that it was being sold online.

Regardless, somehow sedating antihistamines, contaminated with nitazenes were being supplied in his 'patch'. And by getting nitazenes into widely abused 'sleep aids', it was exploding open a new and previously inaccessible market. It made commercial sense.

It was barbaric.

He could round up the dealers but that would only alert the top supplier. He needed more information. He'd talk with Shaun and Sameera again.

But first he wanted to visit the hospital.

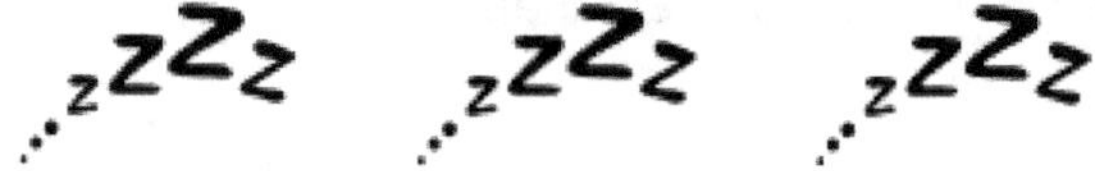

CHAPTER SEVEN

Detective Schmitt stared at the young 'hood', as he lay in his hospital bed.

Eventually, he said *"How'd that happen?"* pointing to the young man's shattered knee. Knowing full well how.

"Don't have to talk to yah", the 'gangsta' smart-mouthed his reply. The police had very little on him. Ancient history only, a few points for speeding and 'due care and attention'.

And he knew it.
"Get well soon hop-along", said Schmitt turning away, "Be seeing you". He winked.

"Whatever," was the sullen reply.

"Good afternoon, Detective", greeted Sameera not unkindly as Detective Schmitt entered her office without knocking. Sameera hoped this was a professional meeting and not about Shaun.

"Hi Sameera. You heard about the shooting no doubt", Sameera nodded. Thinking how blunt and business like Schmitt was today; relieved it wasn't about Shaun.

"Yes", Schmitt continued as he seated himself in front of her desk. *"One gang ripped off the other. One dead at the scene. Later another ended up kneecapped in hospital. Nobody is talking"*.

"I've a suspicion it involves these doctored 'sleep aids'" Schmitt said looking pointedly at Sameera. *"What do you know? Anything new? This is a race against time"*.

"Well, I thought you might tell me about the little girl. Is she ok? Do you have permission for me to see the lab test data?" Sameera asked by way of reply.
"Oh yeah. She's fine, and the parents seem normal enough. Granted permission. An accident and close call. They won't make that mistake again". He said throwing a file marked confidential on her desk. *"Looks like 'sleep aids' and nitazenes again. But you're the expert"*.

Sameera let silence descend as she read the medical file and paid close attention to the initial toxicology report.

"You're quite correct" she said shattering the moment.

"Our third nitazene contaminated 'sleep aid' incident".

"Let's go see the Taylor family", Schmitt said and abruptly stood up.

The meeting over.

The poor Taylor family had little to help progress their investigation. Emma had bought 'sleep aids' from what she understood to be a reputable online website.

Probably a clone of a big-name brand.
She'd been duped like millions of others. Legitimate online pharmacy websites were taken down in a coordinated assault with denial-of-service attacks and concurrently replaced with superbly crafted, but fraudulent clones selling counterfeit drugs.

Sameera and Pete left them to try and rebuild their family.

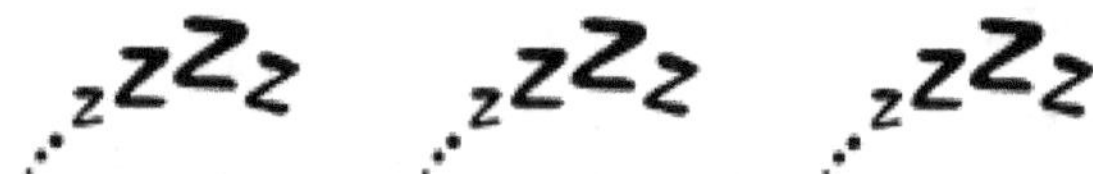

The Russo-China cyber warfare attacks on the West intensified, while governments were content to keep it from the headlines.

The public only began to appreciate the scale of the problem when the police failed to respond to one national emergency after another. Leaders across the Western World called for calm and apologised on public address systems reminiscent of Covid-19 pandemic updates.

Rioting in every major city began, while residents shivered in their homes with extensive black outs during winter months. Thieves walked brazenly down the street after looting shops and homes in broad daylight. Law and order evaporated. Vigilante groups sprung up to fill the void left by the absence of the police. Schools closed and online classes were only proposed after months of chaos. Two more weeks passed, and national emergencies were called, curfews imposed in the hours of darkness, all enforced by the military. Martial law was imposed. All police officers were issued firearms.

The success of the cyber warfare campaign, dispersal of already stretched national militaries, and the crime wave fuelled by harnessing the insomnia epidemic with nitazene addiction, forced a UN Security Council meeting.

Sameera like many millions of others was deep-down tired. She wasn't sleeping well at all. Sleep onset insomnia and waking way too early. Her mental health was suffering as a result. She was starting to doubt herself.

One thing was certain: she wasn't buying 'sleep aids.' Pete Schmitt ran on his treadmill. It was no longer possible nor safe to run in the dark mornings before work. Even for him, a 6-foot 10-inch-tall police officer. He appreciated the need for exercise to support his mental health.

And ran harder.

Pete and Sameera had established a pattern of meeting at 10am every Tuesday in her office. They'd review each other's progress and discuss their next steps.

Pete now reported into COBRA (the Cabinet Office Briefing Room A) having been recognised for his department's prompt response to the crime wave created by the public health disaster, that was the insomnia nitazene catastrophe.

Sameera and Schmitt were closer now to identifying how the counterfeit drugs had entered the grey market for pharmaceuticals. It was all part of a Russo-Chinese strategy to weaponise sleep disorders, sabotage mental health on a scale never before seen, and stretch the military internally such that coordinated, international action would be negligible or impossible.

The EU had declared itself bankrupt. Quantitative easing, and trillions that would never be repaid, brought the bureaucrats back to work.

Ukraine was now a province of Russia. Finland, Romania and Moldova were annexed without so much as a murmur and talk of the reemergence of the USSR didn't seem bizarre.

While Taiwan was quietly absorbed without a shot fired. Western leaders rattled their sabres and talked tough. It had all been predicted, and true to form, they were just as impotent as expected.

The UN couldn't agree a response. They issued the classic fudge of a meaningless statement. The US then imposed further and tougher sanctions. Banning all but emergency, international travel.

'Fortress US' emerged as a slogan.

Shaun was discharged from hospital and police proceedings quietly dropped. Insufficient resources and insufficient prison capacity. And 'surprisingly' they had run out of electronic tags.

Again.

Although 'a stern talking to' with a proper scary Detective Schmitt was enough for most people.

And Doris, her MBE pinned to her blouse, plugged her novel 'The Don't Care Home' on TV. Explaining how the hero (herself of course) spotted the 'sleep aid' crisis before anyone else.

Sameera and Pete tracked down the Big Boss by following the money. When Pete was finally sure he couldn't act. They didn't have the manpower, and he'd need a court order. Etc., etc. the usual paper chase.

So, he went alone. Broke the curfew and entered the arrogantly unguarded mansion. No one would be stupid enough to attack the Big Boss. Except Pete.

Pete levelled his Glock at the head of the crime syndicate boss. Dead looking eyes stared back at him. Glancing down he saw the black double-mouths of a sawn-off shotgun pointing directly at his chest.

Stalemate. The seconds dragged out.

A shot and retort from the surrounding walls.

A body collapsed.

It was over.

About the author

KARL OPUS

As a respected scientist and expert in the field of sleep, I have spent decades helping people with sleep disorders. Writing under the pseudonym, Karl Opus, I have ventured into the world of fiction to explore these themes in a creative and thought-provoking way.

Using a pseudonym allows me to maintain a clear distinction between my scientific work and fictional writing. This separation is essential to protect my professional scientific reputation and ensure that my research and expertise are evaluated independently from this fictional (and I hope fun) story.

I certainly enjoyed creating it!

www.karlopus.com

www.ingramcontent.com/pod-product-compliance
Lightning Source LLC
Chambersburg PA
CBHW052337150726
47998CB00018B/2384